Extreme Stunts

By Ace Landers
Illustrated by Dave White

SCHOLASTIC INC.

ISBN 978-0-545-44463-7

12 11 10 9 8 7 6 5 4 3 2 1   12 13 14 15 16 17/0

Printed in the U.S.A.   40
First printing, September 2012

Meet Team Hot Wheels! They are the most fearless drivers in the world!

The team trains at the Hot Wheels Test Facility.

They test the biggest stunts there.

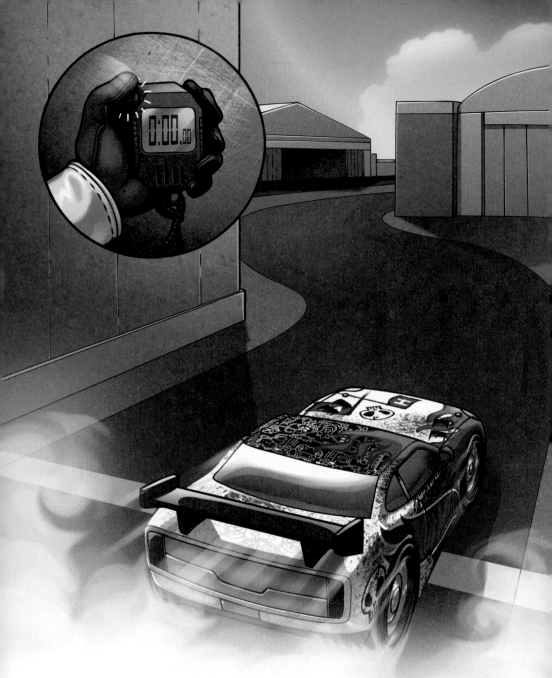

What is Team Green's top speed?

The green driver whips
around the track.

But this course has some
surprises along the way.

He drives fast and thinks faster!

Will the barrels slow him down?

Look out for that truck!

The green driver zooms
around it. He never
loses control!

He crosses the finish line with time to spare!

How daring is Team Red?

The red driver jumps over an airplane!

He flips and flies
through the air!

He lands on a moving truck's ramp.

That was one extreme jump!

Can Team Blue do a perfect trick?

The blue driver will spin
in circles way up high.

It's time to give it some gas!

The blue driver spins as fast as he can without falling off the platform.

He's getting as close to the edge as he can!

Now the blue driver shifts into reverse. He's spinning backward!

Way to go, Team Blue!

How powerful is Team Yellow?

Strong enough to handle this jump. These big wheels love big stunts.

The yellow driver speeds down the steep ramp.

Then he soars through the air.

He just landed the farthest jump ever!

Great work, Team Hot Wheels!